TOO TIGHT, BENITO!

To Margrete, thanks for all the footsteps, love Janeen and Benito.

For Sophie and Alastair—JR

Little Hare Books
8/21 Mary Street, Surry Hills
NSW 2010 AUSTRALIA

www.littleharebooks.com

Copyright © text Janeen Brian 2008
Copyright © illustrations Judith Rossell 2008

First published 2008
Reprinted 2009

National Library of Australia
Cataloguing-in-Publication entry

Brian, Janeen.
Too tight, Benito / author, Janeen Brian; illustrator, Judith Rossell.
Surry Hills, N.S.W. : Little Hare Books, 2008.
978 1 921049 86 6 (hbk.)
For pre-school age.
Rossell, Judith.
A823.3

Designed by Bernadette Gethings
Produced by Pica Digital, Singapore
Printed through Phoenix Offset
Printed in Shen Zhen, Guangdong Province, China, November 2009

6 5 4 3 2

TOO TIGHT, BENITO!

Janeen Brian and Judith Rossell

LITTLE HARE

www.littleharebooks.com

The leaves were falling.
It was Benito Bear's last romp
before crawling into his cubby-hole
to sleep for the winter.

But when he tried to wriggle
inside his cubby-hole,

he got no
more than...

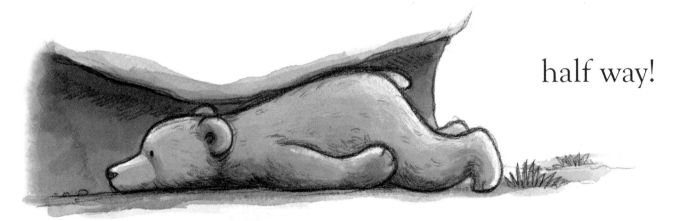

half way!

He could no longer curl up,
or roll around, or stretch out flat.

'I'll have to find a new cubby-hole,'
said Benito Bear.

'A bigger one!'

He headed across the clearing
and found an otter's burrow beside a stream.

But it wasn't a cubby-hole for a bear.
'Too wet,' said Benito, and on he walked.

He found a woodpecker's hole
in a tree, and a rabbit burrow
behind a log.

But they weren't cubby-holes for a bear.

'Too noisy,' said Benito.

'Too crowded.'

And on he walked.

He found an ant hole and a lizard hole,
but no cubby-hole for a bear.

'Too small,' said Benito.

He found an owl hole and a fox hole.

'Too high,' said Benito.

'Too smelly.'

Benito Bear crept into the forest.

He tiptoed further and deeper until
all around him were snappity twigs
and damp leaves, sky-high trees and
swaying shadows.

Benito Bear stopped.
He looked one way and
then the other.
He didn't know where
he was. And he didn't
like where he was.

Then he saw a hole.

Benito Bear dived inside,
away from the snappity twigs and
damp leaves, the sky-high trees
and swaying shadows.

This hole wasn't too wet,
too noisy or too crowded.
It wasn't too high or small or smelly.

This hole was good for
curling up,

and rolling around,

and stretching out flat.

It was a cubby-hole for a bear!

Benito looked up.
He looked from side to side.
He saw darkness all around.

Darkness where things might slither.
Darkness where things might hiss.
Darkness where things might
flap or snap or snarl.

Benito Bear scrambled back
out of the hole.

He ran across the snappity
twigs and damp leaves,
past the sky-high trees
and swaying shadows,
past the log and
the stream.

At last he dived into the safety of
his own, old cubby-hole.

And got stuck!

Benito Bear wriggled.
He squirmed.

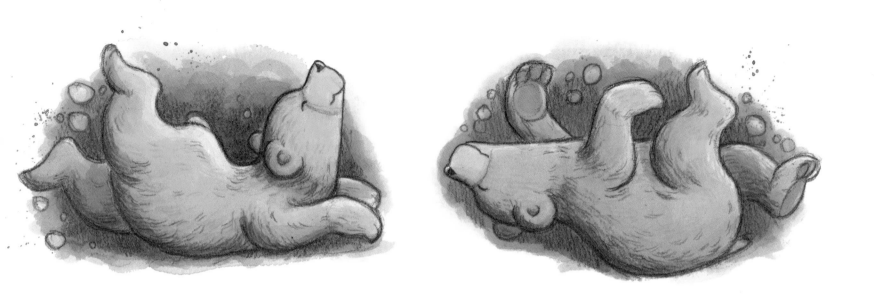

Dirt fell down all around.

Then Benito Bear dug.
He dug wide and deep.
He dug deeper and wider.
He dug until...

...he could crawl all the way inside.

Then he curled up,

rolled around,

and stretched out flat.

Benito's too-small cubby-hole
was now a just-right,
not-too-tight
Benito Bear cubby-hole

with just enough room...

...for one more.